The Adventures of PARKER THE PULI

Balboa Press books may be ordered through booksellers or by contacting:

Balboa Press
A Division of Hay House
1663 Liberty Drive
Bloomington, IN 47403
www.balboapress.com.au
AU TFN: 1 800 844 925 (Toll Free inside Australia)
AU Local: 0283 107 086 (+61 2 8310 7086 from outside Australia)

Because of the dynamic nature of the Internet, any web addresses or
links contained in this book may have changed since publication and may
no longer be valid. The views expressed in this work are solely those
of the author and do not necessarily reflect the views of the publisher,
and the publisher hereby disclaims any responsibility for them.

Any people depicted in stock imagery provided by Getty Images are
models, and such images are being used for illustrative purposes only.
Certain stock imagery © Getty Images.

Interior Image Credit: Tracie Buckley

ISBN: 978-1-5043-2313-0 (sc)
ISBN: 978-1-5043-2312-3 (e)

Print information available on the last page.

Balboa Press rev. date: 11/26/2020

BALBOA.PRESS
A DIVISION OF HAY HOUSE

The Adventures of PARKER THE PULI

Book 2

TOGETHER, FRIENDS ALWAYS WIN

—FIONA KNIGHT—

The autumn sun was shining through the trees when Parker the Puli woke up and decided that he wanted to go to the park with some of his friends. It was going to be a good day!

Parker barked, "Good Morning", to his Mum and trotted out of the blue front door. He then made his way down the street, looking forward to greeting his friends and heading to the park to play.

As Parker walked towards the park, Daisy the Basset Hound whimpered that some of the bigger dogs at the park hadn't been nice to her. Parker just barked, "Well we will be together and we will have fun anyway". Daisy picked up her ears off the ground and followed Parker towards the park.

As they both continued down the street towards the park, they bumped into Turbo the Rottweiler. Turbo was also off to the park with his new ball that he had been given yesterday for his birthday when he turned four. All three pups became excited at the chance to play together with a new ball.

When the three friends got to the park, they could see the bigger dogs standing around near the pond. As Parker, Daisy and Turbo walked through the gates the three bigger dogs came running toward the pups. They stopped and stood in front of the friends.

It was a big Shepherd named Duke with his two Shepherd friends. Duke barked at Turbo, "You need to give me that ball!". Turbo sighed deeply and looked very sad then went to give the Shepherd his new ball. But Parker barked, "STOP, it's not your ball Duke!", and moved close next to Turbo, standing side by side.

Duke looked Parker up and down, then growled, "What are you going to do about it Mop Dog! I want that ball!". When Daisy and Turbo saw Parker standing up for his friends, they decided enough was enough - they were all in this together!

14

Both the pups stepped forward, to stand either side of Parker and then barked, "Go away Duke, you're a bully and we are not sharing our ball with you - so go away now!". Duke the Shepherd looked at the three pups in shock then walked away slowly with his two friends.

Yeah we did it!" All three pups yelped with glee, smiling happily with their tongues hanging out. Daisy, Parker, and Turbo then played for the whole morning in the park with Turbo's ball, sharing and taking turns at throwing the ball to one another. They had a great morning bouncing around and barking with joy, as together, friends always win.

Printed in the United States
By Bookmasters